POLIDORI   CLAIRE   BYRON

SHELLEY   MARY   THE MONSTER

For the kids who love to daydream and imagine. — L.B.

For Tara Walker — J.S.

TEXT COPYRIGHT © 2018 BY LINDA BAILEY
ILLUSTRATIONS COPYRIGHT © 2018 BY JÚLIA SARDÀ

Tundra Books, an imprint of Penguin Random House Canada Young Readers, a Penguin Random House Company

LIBRARY AND ARCHIVES CANADA CATALOGUING IN PUBLICATION

Bailey, Linda, 1948-, author
Mary who wrote Frankenstein / by Linda Bailey ; illustrated by Júlia Sardà.
Issued in print and electronic formats.
ISBN 978-1-77049-559-3 (hardcover).—ISBN 978-1-77049-561-6 (epub)

1. Shelley, Mary Wollstonecraft, 1797-1851-Juvenile literature.
2. Authors, English-19th century-Biography-Juvenile literature.
I. Sardà, Júlia, 1987-, illustrator II. Title.

PR5398.B34 2018   J823'.7   C2017-905562-3   C017-905563-1

Published simultaneously in the United States of America by Tundra Books of Northern New York, an imprint of Penguin Random House Canada Young Readers, a Penguin Random House Company

LIBRARY OF CONGRESS CONTROL NUMBER: 2017951209

Edited by Tara Walker
Designed by CS Richardson and John Martz
The artwork in this book was rendered digitally and in watercolor.
The text was set in Historical Fell Type Roman.

I am very grateful for the help of Dr. Maggie Kilgour, Molson Professor of English Language and Literature, McGill University, Montreal, who kindly reviewed this book and provided invaluable feedback and thoughtful insights. Any errors, omissions or inaccuracies are my own.

Huge thanks to the incomparable Tara Walker for bringing her editorial excellence to this book — and many more thanks to the wonderful team at Tundra Books, especially Margot Blankier, Liz Kribs, John Martz and Peter Phillips.

— Linda Bailey

PRINTED AND BOUND IN CHINA

www.penguinrandomhouse.ca

1 2 3 4 5   22 21 20 19 18

Penguin
Random House
TUNDRA BOOKS
tundra

MARY

WHO WROTE
FRANKENSTEIN

WRITTEN BY
Linda Bailey

ILLUSTRATED BY
Júlia Sardà

tundra

HOW DOES
A STORY BEGIN?

Sometimes it begins
with a dream.

Here is Mary. She's a dreamer. The kind of girl who wanders alone, who stares at clouds, who imagines things that never were. Mary has a name for her daydreams. She calls them "castles in the air."

Mary loves stories too. She tries to write the kind that she reads. But the stories she sees in daydreams are the most thrilling of all.

And where does she go to read and dream? She goes to a graveyard and sits at her mother's grave.

Mary's mother was a great thinker. She wrote books to say that women should have the same rights as men. She died when Mary was only eleven days old.

Can you miss someone you've never known?

Mary does.

Mary's father is also a thinker. He taught Mary to read by tracing the letters on her mother's gravestone. Mary loves her father, but he can be strict and stiff. And when he's upset with her, he grows cold and silent . . . until she cries.

Before very long, he marries again.
Mary doesn't like the new wife.
The new wife doesn't like Mary, either.

Famous people visit their London home. Philosophers, artists, scientists, writers.

One night at a party, a writer named Samuel Taylor Coleridge recites a strange, eerie poem — *The Rime of the Ancient Mariner*. Mary *loves* such poems. But she has been sent to bed.

She wants so badly to listen that she hides behind a sofa. She and her stepsister shiver with fear at the spine-tingling tale of a ship full of ghosts.

For the rest of her life, Mary will remember this night. And she will *never* forget that poem.

Mary is angry and unhappy at home, and she shows it. By the time she's fourteen, she has become a Big Problem. Her father sends her away to live with a family of strangers in Scotland.

The family is kind. Mary likes them. As she wanders the barren hills, she can let her imagination roam free. But at sixteen, when she returns to her family, she is still a Big Problem.

And what does she do next?

She becomes an even Bigger Problem. She runs away with a brilliant young poet. Her stepsister, Claire, goes along too. The poet's name is Percy Bysshe Shelley. Like Mary, he's a dreamer.

Mary's family is horrified!

With very little money, the young people travel in Europe by horse and donkey, and on foot. They also take a boat down the Rhine River. One day the boat ties up near a ruined castle. It's called Castle Frankenstein.

Such an interesting name!

Does it stick in Mary's mind?

But it's on their next trip together, eighteen months later, that things get *really* interesting. On this trip, Mary, Shelley and Claire travel to Switzerland, where they make friends with a famous poet.

Lord Byron is the most famous poet in the world.
(He's also famous for being handsome.) He is staying in a
beautiful house beside Lake Geneva. On breezy spring
days, they can go sailing!

But summer brings mysterious storms. Dark clouds rumble and churn.

One evening comes the wildest storm of all. Lightning rips the sky. Thunder booms! Rain lashes the house beside the lake.

Inside, five people sit huddled beside the fire. Two young women. Two poets. A medical doctor.

The doctor is a friend of Lord Byron. His name is John Polidori, and he loves to write.

What can such people do on a night like this?

Only one thing.

It's a night made for . . .

Ghost stories!

Byron opens a book of ghoulish stories called *Fantasmagoriana*. In the flickering firelight, he begins to read.

As the others listen, their mouths go dry. Their scalps prickle. Their hair stands up. They can almost *see* the ghostly apparitions dancing on the walls.

Such is the power of a scary story on a stormy night.

At the end of the evening, Byron
suggests a contest. "We will each write
a ghost story," he says.
Whose will be best?

Remember now, who is in this room.
Two brilliant poets, one of them famous.
A doctor. Two very young women.
Mary is only eighteen.

And what happens next? Well, according to Mary . . .
Shelley and Byron begin their stories right away,
and so does Polidori.

"Do you have an idea?" they ask Mary.

"No," she says.

Every day, they ask her again. "Have you thought of a story?"

"No," she says.

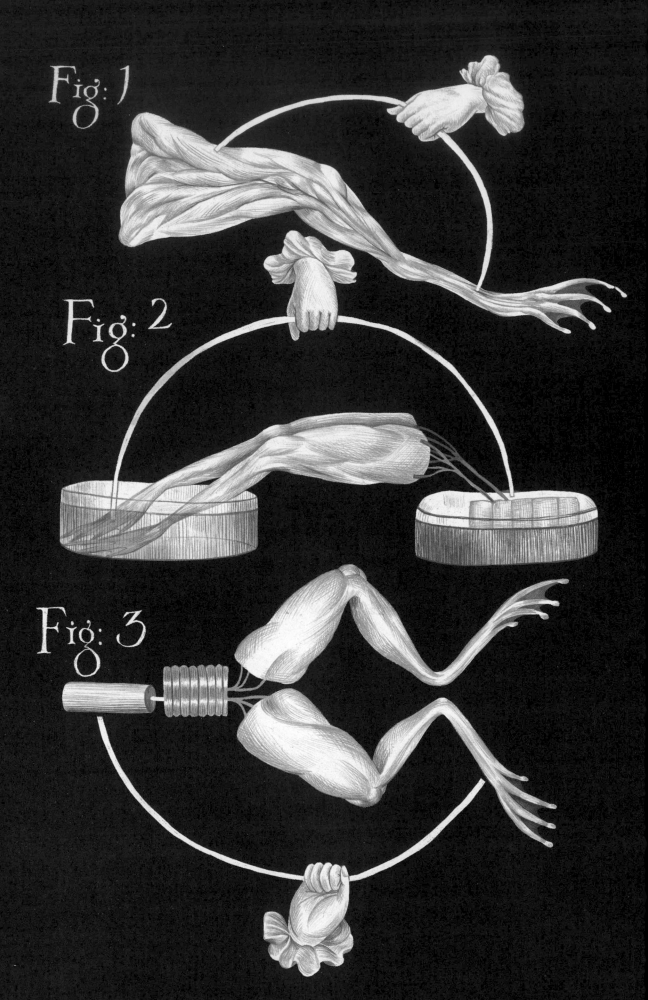

Fig: 1

Fig: 2

Fig: 3

Shelley and Byron get bored. They stop writing stories. They start to plan a sailing tour around the lake instead. And they talk one evening — as they've been talking all summer — about new discoveries in science. Exciting experiments! Electricity can make the muscles of a dead frog twitch. Could it bring a dead creature to life?

The idea is both thrilling and frightening.

Mary listens. Later, she goes to bed. But she can't fall asleep. Instead, in that strange, lost time between wake and sleep, she has a kind of daydream. She sees a hideous monster, made of dead body parts, stretched out — and coming to life! The scientist who made the monster is so scared at what he's done, he runs away.

Mary opens her eyes, frightened. She tries to forget what she imagined. She tries to think up a ghost story instead.

And then, with a sudden jolt of excitement, she understands. She has already *found* her ghost story! The monster coming to life. *That* is the story she will write. Finally, she has her idea.

The next morning, she sits down and writes these words: "It was on a dreary night of November . . ."

The writing of *Frankenstein* has begun.

It takes nine more months of daydreaming and writing for Mary to finish her story. Two publishers say no to publishing it. A third publisher finally agrees to make it into a book.

The first people who read *Frankenstein* are sure it was written by Percy Shelley. They don't believe young Mary could have done it! How could a girl like her come up with such a story?

But maybe *you* know.

She wrote a scary story about a scientist named Victor Frankenstein who brought a dead creature to life and then became frightened at what he had done.

Scary story. Frankenstein. Dead creature. Scientific change. Where did such ideas come from? And how did they come together?

In a writer's imagination.

In a dream.

Writers dream stories, awake and asleep.

Over two hundred years have passed since that night beside the lake. And everywhere around the world, people know Mary's book. It has become a legend! It may be the greatest scary story of all time.

And now you know how it started . . .

It began with a girl named Mary. She liked to daydream and imagine.

And she grew up to write *Frankenstein*.

AUTHOR'S NOTE

Mary Shelley (1797—1851) wrote her extraordinary novel *Frankenstein; or, The Modern Prometheus* when she was only eighteen years old. The book that she wrote was astonishing. But no less remarkable perhaps is the story of how she wrote it.

This story-behind-the-story was told by Mary herself in an "Author's Introduction" she wrote in 1831, thirteen years after the book was first published. Mary wanted to explain the book's origins in order to answer a question she had often been asked: "How I, then a young girl, came to think of and to dilate upon so very hideous an idea?" In her Introduction, she described not only her creative process during the writing of *Frankenstein*, but also her early and adolescent imagination. It's a fascinating read.

When I reread this Introduction a few years back, I wondered whether it might make a picture book — and as I began to explore the many fine adult biographies of Mary Shelley that have appeared in recent years, I was quickly enthralled. Mary's life, by both accident and choice, was rich with drama. It was filled with the kind of powerful themes that are written again and again in fiction.

I discovered, in fact, that there were actually *many* stories within the story of Mary's life and creativity.

One is the story of a motherless child. Mary's mother, Mary Wollstonecraft, was an early hero of feminism and the illustrious author of *A Vindication of the Rights of Woman*. She died eleven days after Mary's birth. Mary's father, philosopher William Godwin, remarried after Wollstonecraft's death, but young Mary's love and loyalty were always reserved for the mother she had never known.

Another thread running through Mary's life is the story of a powerful imagination. Throughout her childhood, Mary's refuge from unhappiness was a vivid fantasy life. As a child, she "scribbled" and indulged in "waking dreams." As an adolescent on the bleak Scottish coast, she escaped into "flights of imagination" in which she was happy to "people the hours" with creatures of her own fancy.

And of course, Mary's story is also very much a love story — filled with passion, rebellion, sacrifice and loss. From beginning to end, her relationship with poet Percy Bysshe Shelley (whom she married in late 1816) was tumultuous and often painful. Yet it was also enriching. As writers, Mary and Shelley inspired one another, and Shelley acted as both editor and agent for Mary's manuscript of *Frankenstein*.

Sadly, Mary's life was also a story of people who died too young. There were so many early deaths. Her mother, of course. But Mary's children too. Mary and Shelley had four children together, one of whom, a baby, was with them at Lake Geneva in the care of a Swiss nursemaid. All of these children, except for the last, died tragically early in childhood. Also among those who died too soon were Mary's fellow participants in that night of ghost stories. Percy Bysshe Shelley drowned in a sailing accident at age twenty-nine. Lord Byron died of fever at age thirty-six in a war for Greek freedom. John Polidori committed suicide at twenty-five. Only the two women, Mary and Claire, survived into middle age.

To readers of *Frankenstein*, of course, the most gripping story about Mary is one of literary creativity — the tale of the inspirational evening of ghost stories, culminating in Lord Byron's challenge and Mary's response. It's such a great story — might it be too good to be strictly true? Some scholars point out discrepancies in Mary's 1831 Introduction compared with other reports of that time. (Sadly, there is little reliable evidence left.) It's possible that after thirteen years, Mary forgot details. It's also possible that Mary, a brilliant

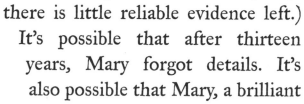

writer of fiction, may have done some judicious editing to create a more dramatic tale. (She definitely "wrote out" her stepsister Claire, an ongoing source of tension in her life.)

But if the details are fuzzy, Mary's story of *Frankenstein*'s origins rings loud and true, at least to me, in terms of the writing process. She tells how, after a slow start, she found herself one night — on the verge of sleep — in the grip of a powerful imagining. A vision? A nightmare? Or perhaps simply a more adult version of the "waking dreams" she had experienced all through childhood? With eyes closed, she saw a succession of vivid, horrific images. The vision she saw — of a scientist staring down at a "creature" he had formed from dead human body parts and was now bringing to life — shocked her profoundly.

Her shock, however, was *not* so profound that she didn't quickly see the story possibilities. Remembering Byron's challenge, she recognized that here — *here!* — was her ghost story. She began to conceive a tale about these characters.

To some, Mary's strange vision may sound like magic. Writers of fiction, however, are likely to recognize the experience she described — that trancelike state in which characters seem to simply appear and a story seems to tell itself. Fiction writers will also recognize the "chaos," as Mary called it, of sources that feed a growing novel — in her case, the Prometheus legend, discussions of galvanism, folklore, gothic novels, a castle in Germany, a hike on an Alpine glacier, Coleridge's *The Rime of the Ancient Mariner* and, more generally, a lifelong habit of voracious and intensive reading.

It took Mary nine months of hard, disciplined work to complete a first draft.

Frankenstein was published in 1818. After a modest start, it achieved great success, partly because of the popularity of the theater productions that were inspired by the book. These plays, like most of the movies that followed, changed and simplified Mary's original *Frankenstein*.

But the book flourished and lasted, and Mary's story eventually became one of creative breakthrough — perhaps even the start of a new genre. *Frankenstein; or, The Modern Prometheus* is widely considered to be the first modern novel of science fiction.

Finally, a P.S. — in this case standing for "Polidori's story." Byron's doctor also had literary ambitions. He was the only member of the group besides Mary who actually finished and published a story in response to the famous challenge. Inspired by a fragment of Lord Byron's writing, Polidori wrote a story called "The Vampyre." It wasn't a great story. But its portrayal of a romantic, aristocratic vampire helped to inspire a later, better vampire tale — Bram Stoker's *Dracula*. It's possible therefore that the evening that inspired the greatest monster of science fiction may have also helped to inspire the greatest vampire of the horror genre.

No wonder so many readers over the years have been gripped. A dark and stormy night, five bright, young, unconventional minds — and one of the most fascinating stories of literary creativity ever told.

At the center of it all was Mary Shelley. She was only eighteen, and she wrote *Frankenstein*.

SOURCES

Darrow, Sharon. *Through the Tempests Dark and Wild: A Story of Mary Shelley, Creator of Frankenstein*. Cambridge, MA: Candlewick Press, 2003.

Gordon, Charlotte. *Romantic Outlaws: The Extraordinary Lives of Mary Wollstonecraft and Her Daughter Mary Shelley*. New York: Random House, 2015.

Hay, Daisy. *Young Romantics: The Shelleys, Byron and Other Tangled Lives*. London: Bloomsbury, 2010.

Holmes, Richard. *The Age of Wonder: How the Romantic Generation Discovered the Beauty and Terror of Science*. London: HarperPress, 2008.

Hoobler, Dorothy and Thomas. *The Monsters: Mary Shelley and the Curse of Frankenstein*. New York: Little Brown, 2006.

Montillo, Roseanne. *The Lady and Her Monsters: A Tale of Dissections, Real-Life Dr. Frankensteins, and the Creation of Mary Shelley's Masterpiece*. New York: William Morrow, 2013.

Seymour, Miranda. *Mary Shelley*. London: John Murray, 2000.

Shelley, Mary. *Frankenstein; or, The Modern Prometheus*. Ed. Maurice Hindle. New York: Penguin, 2003.

———. *Selected Letters of Mary Wollstonecraft Shelley*. Ed. Betty T. Bennett. Baltimore: John Hopkins University Press, 1995.

Spark, Muriel. *Mary Shelley: A Biography*. Manchester: Carcanet, 2013. First published 1988 by Constable and Company.

Stott, Andrew McConnell. *The Vampyre Family: Passion, Envy and the Curse of Byron*. Edinburgh: Canongate, 2013. (Also available as *The Poet and the Vampyre: The Curse of Byron and the Birth of Literature's Greatest Monsters*. New York: Pegasus Books, 2014.)

Sunstein, Emily W. *Mary Shelley: Romance and Reality*. Boston: Little, Brown, 1989.

Todd, Janet M. *Death and the Maidens: Fanny Wollstonecraft and the Shelley Circle*. Berkeley, CA: Counterpoint, 2007.

Illustration of the Georgian-era London, England street scene: Based on an 1850 engraving of Somers Town by Joseph Swain.

Image accompanying Author's Note: *Mary Wollstonecraft Shelley* by Richard Rothwell, c. 1840. © National Portrait Gallery, London.